THE
BAREFOOT BOOK OF
FATHER
— AND —
SON
TALES

For John and his son Benedict
— J. E.-S.
For my brother, Joff — H.C.

Barefoot Collections
an imprint of
Barefoot Books
41 Schermerhorn Street,
Suite 145, Brooklyn,
New York
NY 11201-4845

Library of Congress Cataloging-in-Publication Data is available on request.

ISBN 1 902283 32 5
Graphic design by Design / Section, Frome
Color separation by Grafiscan, Verona
This book has been printed on 100% acid-free paper
Printed in Hong Kong by South Sea International Press
1 3 5 7 9 8 6 4 2

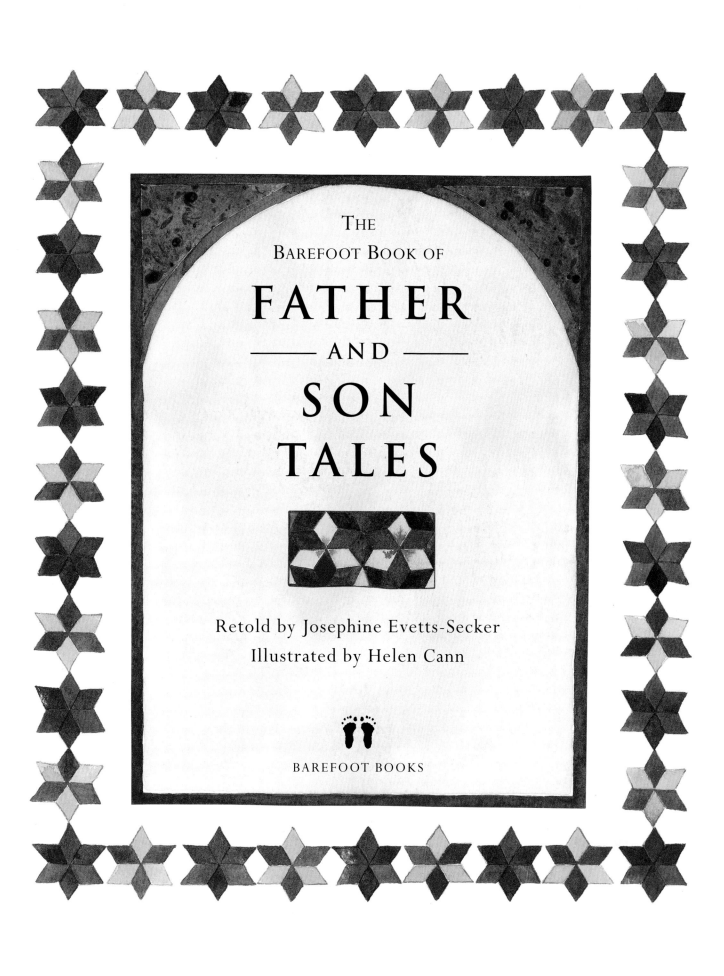

THE
BAREFOOT BOOK OF
FATHER
— AND —
SON
TALES

Retold by Josephine Evetts-Secker

Illustrated by Helen Cann

BAREFOOT BOOKS

CONTENTS

FOREWORD

This collection of stories illuminates the father–son bond. The tales explore the love and expectation that form and complicate father–son relationships, helping or hindering growth into maturity and the development of genuine masculine strength.

As a boy starts to mature, he needs to strengthen the bond with the father, whose expectations must be challenging but not overwhelming. The tests fathers set their sons, consciously or unconsciously, form the growing child and can determine his future sense of identity and potency. If the boy does not learn strength, he will either feel defeated or use force instead of strength to assert himself.

Some of the fathers in these tales are powerful, loving and generous, even indulgent; but they are also rash and foolish, incompetent, feeble, poor or sick. Even when they are potent, they are inevitably aging and they belong to an old order that must be renewed or even replaced.

When the stories feature more than one son, the fathers allow some competitiveness between brothers; but this is rebuked when it fosters envy or hatred. Such competition is usually for the father's affection, approval or his crown. The tales do not tolerate fathers competing with their sons, though sons can admire fathers and be motivated to fulfil their hopes.

Good fathers offer their sons challenges but with empathy and realism. Weakness is not despised but supported so that it may become an opportunity for growth. The Chippewa story, "The First Corn," demonstrates this fertile bond, which initiates the discovery of sweetcorn.

As they make their passage into adult life, the sons carry with them the influence of fathers, foster-fathers and ancestors; they seek out fire gods and sea giants and meet magical manikins; they travel into the forests, to the bottom of the sea, into the underworld or up into the skies.

They also learn how to reconnect with feminine values first experienced through the mother, values that cannot be excluded from masculine thinking and behavior. Often the sons reach out to the feminine in the form of a bride. At first she may appear in animal form, for animals can relate ambitious young men back to instinctual life.

As they travel – and each one's progress takes him on a journey – the sons of these stories interact with the world in accordance with, or reaction against, their fathers' influence. The Siberian folk tradition insists that "everything has a voice." Each son must learn to hear this voice and enter into dialogue with the rest of creation, or he will simply attempt to master it – a masculine fault in many tales.

Mighty deeds are not needed when magic can bring about the desired result. This magic is often simply behaving in the right way, being in the right place at the right time and, most importantly, having the right attitude. Magic is sometimes simple tact or kindness. This is what sons must learn.

At no time have we perhaps been more in need of assistance in understanding what it is to nourish the paternal, without falling into patriarchy. Father–son relationships are the same across geographic and temporal boundaries and in all of them we recognize the same successes and failures. The tales in this collection help to remind us of things we have forgotten or show us things we have overlooked.

Josephine Evetts-Secker

DAEDALUS AND ICARUS

GREEK

Long ago, in ancient Greece, there lived a very clever man named Daedalus who was famous as a sculptor, carpenter and engineer. Everyone who saw his inventions was amazed and before long his fame spread far across the Mediterranean Sea, from his home in Athens to the island of Crete. At that time Crete was an extremely rich and powerful kingdom, with many smaller islands in the Mediterranean under its control. It was ruled by a powerful king and queen, Minos and Pasiphae, who lived in a very grand palace in the city of Knossos. When Minos heard about Daedalus, he sent him an invitation to come and work for the royal household in Crete. Daedalus did not know it, but Minos wanted him to build a massive labyrinth for a strange monster, half-bull and half-man, which had been born to the king and the queen. They were ashamed and afraid of this creature, whom they called the Minotaur, so they wanted to hide it.

Daedalus set to work to design an intricate set of pathways that wound around, bending back on themselves and changing direction unexpectedly. At the core of the labyrinth he left a space for the Minotaur to rampage freely.

Minos was delighted. "How marvellous is your creation, Daedalus!" he exclaimed. "You are indeed the most cunning designer in all of Greece. No one else could have created such a remarkable labyrinth. How glad I am to have you here on my prosperous island. You must stay here forever and work for me. We will become famous, my friend!"

But although life in Minos and Pasiphae's palace was extremely comfortable, and although they had everything they needed, Daedalus and Icarus soon began to feel like prisoners. For Minos was aware that only Daedalus knew how to reach the heart of the labyrinth and he did not want such an important secret to go beyond the shores of his island. To keep Daedalus happy, he gave him a magnificent workshop and offered him as many apprentices as he needed. He even told Daedalus that he was free to make whatever his heart desired. But once the labyrinth was completed Daedalus began to lose pleasure in his work. Instead he began to dream of returning to the city he had left behind. "Do you remember the streets of Athens, my son?" he would say to Icarus. "How splendid a city it is, with its beautiful buildings and gardens. A city pleasing to all the gods, but especially to Pallas Athene, daughter of Zeus. How I long to enter her temples again."

Icarus had only vague memories of the city but he loved to hear his father's stories. "Tell me about Athens," he would say as they sat watching the sunset, the sea birds swooping over their heads. Separated from them by many miles of ocean, Athens seemed very far away.

Day by day, Daedalus's longing to return home increased, and his son was
borne along by his father's yearning. But Minos would not grant them leave
to sail from the island so they spent their days on the shore watching the ships
enter and leave the harbor of Herakleion.

"If only we were birds!" Icarus cried out. "Then we would be free and could
fly where we liked. We could fly back to Athens!"

Daedalus was suddenly gripped by his son's fantasy. "That's it, Icarus! That
is exactly right! We must learn from the birds themselves."

Now the idea took hold of him and he worked on it every hour, saying
little to Icarus who followed him along the shore, picking up shells and
the odd feather dropped by a bird. Daedalus muttered to himself, then
gestured with his arms and said to Icarus, "Find all the feathers you can,
the smallest and the largest, and bring them to me … And we must save
all our candles too."

At last it became clear to Icarus what his father was planning. Together they
laid the feathers out in wing shapes, arranging them in order of size. When

they had sufficient feathers to make two pairs of wings, they sealed them in place with candle wax and made fastenings with the thongs from their sandals. Icarus loved working with his father, sharing his excitement and feeling useful each time he collected a pile of feathers.

Finally everything was ready. Four shining white wings lay on the ground, more intricately formed than the winding paths of the labyrinth. Holding his breath with excitement, Icarus allowed his father to strap his pair of wings on to his arms and shoulders. "How heavy they are, father!" he exclaimed when they were securely tied.

His father looked worried for a moment and then replied reassuringly, "Once you get into the lift of the wind, you will not feel the weight, my son. The winds will carry you and you will feel as light as the feathers you brought to me."

Icarus helped his father fasten his even larger wings on to his big body, and together they stood on the edge of the cliff, glancing nervously at each other and out into the empty space before them.

"We must hurry now," said Daedalus, "for the men in the harbor might look up and see us and try to stop us leaving. But a few words of warning, Icarus, before we plunge into the air. Remember what I have told you again and again. Do as I do. Follow me. Do not go your own way. The sun will melt your wings if you fly too high and get caught in Apollo's fierce heat. And if you fly too low, the heavy water from Poseidon's ocean will weigh your wings down and pull you into its depths. Do you hear what I say, my boy?"

"Yes, father," Icarus whispered. Suddenly, he felt full of terror. First he looked down into the space between him and the rocks on the shore below. Then he stared up to the huge sky above them and the hot, bright sun. "I will follow you, father, and do as you say."

Daedalus touched his son's feathered arm encouragingly, then, with a cry, leapt into the bright blue void. With the same loud shout, the boy leapt after his father, full of confidence. For a moment they tumbled downwards, till a blast of wind caught them and they hovered briefly in the warm air. Then another blast carried them forward and they found themselves moving smoothly in a current of wind out to sea.

Icarus was exhilarated as he began to use his wings to move himself through the air. Gradually he learned to change direction and to swoop down or rise up in the currents of wind. "How fast I am flying!" he called out. "How high I can fly!" He was by now ahead of his father, forgetting that he had agreed to follow him. "This is how the gulls must feel!" he cried. "This is how the gods must feel!" he thought, with sudden fear. But the joy of flying possessed him once again and he swooped wildly up and down.

Farmers working in the fields beside the ocean saw the two huge birds in

the sky and were surprised. Some felt terror, thinking that they were gods. Others, intent on their plowing, noticed nothing remarkable. In their boats out at sea, some sailors were curious, others were too weary from gazing at the horizon to care very much. Then, suddenly, those on watch saw a great splash: one mighty bird had fallen from the sky.

Daedalus had been calling out to his son for some time, trying to curb his

wildness. But the winds carried his words of warning further and further away till they disappeared into the heavens. Icarus heard nothing and mounted higher and higher, hurling himself through the sky with reckless joy. He did not even feel the warm wax melting down his arms and his back. He knew nothing until he started to plunge headlong into the deep green sea. Then he cried out in terror. But it was all over so quickly …

Daedalus was still flying behind Icarus, so he saw his beloved son tumbling down to the dark sea, like a bird that has been struck by a catapult. He cried out again, but his words were snatched away by the wind. Daedalus knew that he could not stop. He may have escaped from Crete, but he had lost his son in doing so. With a heavy heart, he flew steadily on to the shore of the nearest island. There, he shook off his wings and gazed back out to sea. His son was nowhere to be seen. Overcome with grief, what could he do but shed bitter tears for his lost boy?

And ever since that day the stretch of ocean into which poor Icarus plunged has been named after him – the Icarian Sea.

THE WATER OF LIFE

GERMAN

Long ago and far away there was a king who was dying. His three sons were distressed and wept together in the palace gardens. An old man came up to them and asked them kindly why they were crying. They told him that their father was dying of an illness that none could cure, although everything had been tried and all the physicians in the country had been consulted.

The old man responded, "There is one remedy that you do not know about – the Water of Life. All who drink this are healed. But it is difficult to find."

"Tell me where it is," cried the eldest son, "so that I may search for it."

But the old man could tell him no more. The prince then rushed off to the king to ask to be allowed to go in search of this remedy. At first the king refused, saying, "The road is too dangerous, my son. It is foolish for you to die in trying to save me."

But the prince insisted, thinking that if only he could find this cure, he would become the king's favorite son.

He set out as soon as he could and had not gone far before he met a dwarf who stood in his path and called out, "Where are you going in such haste?"

Extremely irritated, the prince shouted back, "You stupid fool, get out of my way!" and rode on.

The dwarf was so angered by such rude behavior that he wished the prince ill. Before long the young man entered a ravine that grew narrower and narrower so that he could not move or even turn around in it. The mountains had imprisoned him.

Meanwhile the king grew weaker and paler, giving up all hope of seeing his son again. Then the next son implored him to let him also try to find the Water of Life, thinking that if his brother was dead, he would inherit the kingdom.

The king lamented, "I have already lost one son." Nevertheless the second son set off on the route followed by his brother.

Before long he too met the dwarf in his path who asked, "Where are you going in such haste?"

The prince also replied, "You stupid fool, get out of my way!"

The dwarf felt the same anger at this impatient brother and bewitched him so that the mountains trapped him also.

By now the king was even closer to death and the third son begged to be allowed to search for the Water of Life. The king had no energy to refuse so the youngest prince set off and soon encountered the same dwarf who asked, "Where are you going in such haste?"

The prince answered politely, "I am anxious to find the Water of Life so that my father might be cured."

The dwarf then inquired whether the prince knew where the water was to be found, and as the youth sadly shook his head, the dwarf said, "Do not despair, kind prince. I will tell you where you must go. This water springs from a fountain in the grounds of an enchanted castle. I can help you with this gift of an iron staff and these two loaves of bread. The castle doors will open only when struck with this staff. Inside you will find two lions with hungry jaws, but they will be satisfied with this bread if you give it to them. Be sure to get the water from the fountain before midnight, for then the doors will slam shut again."

Gratefully the prince took the gifts and rode to the castle where he did

exactly as the dwarf had instructed him. The doors flew open at the third strike
and the lions quietly took the loaves, enabling him to enter the courtyard.
There he found a magnificent hall where bewitched princes slept. He took
the rings from their fingers together with a sword and another loaf of bread
that he found there. He then entered an inner chamber where he found a
lovely princess who rejoiced to see him.

"You have set me free," she said, "and you may surely marry me in a year's
time." She then told him where he could find the fountain containing the
Water of Life.

After taking water from the fountain, the exhausted prince searched for a
bed where he lay down to sleep, waking only just in time as the clock struck

a quarter to twelve. As he escaped through the entrance to the castle, the clock struck midnight and the doors slammed shut, catching his heel as they closed. The prince cared nothing for his lost heel now that he had found the cure for his father's sickness.

He rode like the wind till he came again upon the dwarf, who said, "You have done well. For with that sword you will defeat great armies and that loaf of bread may be eaten but never consumed."

The prince was reluctant to go home without his brothers, and when the dwarf explained that they were caught in a dark ravine as punishment for their selfishness, the young man felt pity for them. He begged for their release, which the dwarf granted, but with this caution: "Beware of your brothers for they have evil hearts."

Nevertheless the youngest son rejoiced when he saw them and shared all his secrets with them, including the story of the princess whom he would marry at the year's end.

They rode on together and crossed the sea till they came to a kingdom where war and famine raged and the king and his people were in despair. The youngest prince offered the king his sword and his endless loaf so that he could defeat his enemies and feed his people.

Then, taking back the bread and sword, he rode on with his brothers. They traveled through two more kingdoms where the sword and bread were again put to use. Again the kingdoms were spared and the princes continued their journey.

As they set sail across the ocean on their way home, the two older brothers spoke with envy of their young brother: "Since he has found the Water of Life

to cure our father, he will be given the kingdom and we will have nothing!"
So they plotted against him. Finding him asleep in his cabin, they exchanged
the flask of healing water for sea water and took the Water of Life back to the
king themselves.

When the three brothers reached their father's kingdom, the youngest
prince joyfully gave what he believed to be the healing water to his father, but
of course it had no effect. The king became worse after drinking salt water and
the prince was hurt when his brothers accused him of trying to poison their
father. They then produced the healing water and restored the king to health.

The king was full of gratitude to his sons, who started to heap abuse on their
younger brother, claiming for themselves the beautiful bride he had spoken of.
In private they threatened him with his life if he revealed their deception.

Meanwhile the king and his court feared that the youngest prince had
indeed tried to poison his father; he was a danger to the kingdom and must be

destroyed. But the king's huntsman, who had been ordered to kill the prince while hunting in the forest, told the youngest son of the plot against him.

"Dear huntsman, please spare my life!" begged the prince. "I will give you my royal garments in exchange for your old clothes, and I will bear you no ill will, I assure you." So the prince escaped and the huntsman returned to the castle, pretending to have carried out the king's command.

After a time, gold and jewels arrived at the castle as gifts for the youngest prince from the kings whose lands had been saved by his sword and his loaf. On hearing this, the king began to feel ill at ease, wondering if perhaps his son had been innocent after all. He bitterly regretted his hasty decision to destroy him and wept as he spoke of this to the huntsman. Relieved by the king's change of heart, the huntsman told him what had happened in the forest. Joyfully the king announced that his youngest son should be found and brought home.

The princess who had been freed from the enchanted castle had now returned to her palace and ordered that a special road be built, in shining gold, leading up to her gates. "Whoever rides up the center of the road shall be allowed to enter, for he will be my bridegroom. But whoever rides along its sides must not be admitted," she told her people.

The year had passed and the eldest prince set off to claim the princess and her kingdom. When he saw the golden road, he said to himself, "It would be a shame to trample on such a precious road. I will ride on the right side of it." But when he reached the gates he was not allowed to enter.

"You are not the true prince," the men at the gates declared.

The same fate befell the second prince. He tried to enter the palace by riding along the left side of the golden road, and he too was refused entrance.

Meanwhile the youngest son, who had wandered through many kingdoms waiting for the year to end, reached the palace at the appointed time. When he saw the shining road, he said to himself, "What a fitting pathway to my bride!" and, his heart beating wildly, he galloped straight up the center of it.

The gates flew open and the princess stood there in splendor to receive him. Their marriage was celebrated at once, after which the princess told her husband that his father wanted to ask for his forgiveness.

The prince and his bride returned to his father's kingdom and the truth was revealed. His father embraced him and promised him his kingdom. As for the two deceitful sons, they set sail at once for foreign countries, never to return.

THE ROYAL CANDLESTICK

EGYPTIAN

Let me tell you a story I heard long ago.

There was once a merchant who had one much-loved son. Every morning he gave money to his son, saying, "Here is more money. Go and spend it. Don't worry when it is gone. Just ask and I will give you more!"

This endless supply made the boy curious. "Where is this money coming from?" he wondered. "Perhaps my father makes it himself." With that in mind, he made so bold as to ask for a very large amount. "So that I may go off into the world to establish myself in business," he explained.

His father was surprised and answered, "But, my son, why do you need to go away? Surely you have everything here that you could possibly need?"

But his son insisted that he must leave. So the old man gave him the money. In addition his mother gave him some of her jewels, saying, "If ever you are in need, sell some of the jewels from this priceless necklace."

The young man took the money, but he had spent it all before the end of the day. He did not spoil himself with gifts, but he gave all he had to the poor. Soon he was left with nothing except the necklace. "How can I return to my father now I have spent all his money without even starting my business?" he thought. "I must run away for I cannot go back."

He walked on and on till he reached the river bank, where he met a fisherman. "Please cast a line for me," he asked, "to check my luck." The fisherman obliged and when he pulled out his line, there was a tiny brass box at the end of it. The boy reached out to take it but the fisherman refused, saying, "I will not part with this for less than a fortune."

"I have only a precious necklace," the boy replied. The fisherman took the necklace from him and went on with his fishing, while the boy wandered off with his little box. He walked and walked and walked, till he came to a deserted place. He was beginning to feel hungry, but had nothing to eat. "I don't even have any money to buy any food," he realized. "I have spent all that I was given and I have nothing to show for it except this tiny brass box. Now what shall I do?"

After awhile, he decided to open the box. He was amazed to find a tiny manikin there. The little creature said, "I am here to serve you. What would you have me do?"

The boy was bewildered, so the manikin continued, "I am your luck. Ask for what you want and I will provide it for you."

"That's easy," said the boy. "I am hungry. Bring me food."

The boy was instructed to close his eyes and when he opened them again, he saw a table loaded with food. So he ate all he wanted, cleared everything away, picked up his box and resumed his travels.

He walked and walked and walked, till he reached a foreign country. At the border town he found a palace built of human skulls. He kept asking the townspeople why the palace was built in that way, but he could get no reply. Eventually he asked an old woman who sat nearby.

"Old aunt," he began, "please can you tell me why the palace is built of skulls?"

The old woman replied, "It is built that way because the king has a daughter who does not speak. He has offered his kingdom to any young man who will make her talk to him within three days. But he who fails will be beheaded."

The boy consulted the manikin, who agreed to help. "Just put me under the candlestick inside the princess's room and I will make her speak."

The king thought the boy too young to lose his head but he allowed him to try to win his daughter. He put his royal seal on the contract and the boy was taken to the unspeaking maiden. He plied her with greetings and questions but she uttered not a word. She was like a stone statue. While the princess was not looking, the boy slipped the little box with the manikin under the candlestick. Then he turned to the candlestick and said, "Since she won't keep me company, perhaps you will?"

The candlestick replied, "All right, then I'll tell you a story." And it began: "Once upon a time there were three brothers who all wanted to marry the same bride. So they were sent on a journey and told that whoever brought back the greatest riches would have the bride. They traveled together till they

came to a place where three roads branched off, and each brother went down a different road. The one who went down the road of no return discovered the water of life. The one who took the safe road found a flying carpet, and the brother who took the middle road found a mirror that could show all that was happening in the world. When they met up again, the mirror showed them that the girl was dying. Hopping on to the flying carpet, they rushed back to her house and the first brother gave her the water of life, which revived her instantly."

At this point the candlestick asked the listening boy, "Who do you think should win the bride? For without the mirror they could not have known she was dying; without the carpet they could not have flown home in time and given her the water of life which saved her."

The boy at once said, "She must marry the one who revived her with the water of life, of course."

But the unspeaking princess interrupted, "No, no. Glory be to Allah that we are such curious beings! Without the mirror they would not have seen her condition and would not have rushed to her." To the amazement of the judges, she went on chattering about the story. So they decided to wait to see what happened the next day before telling the king. After they had left, the boy fell asleep. The princess tried to make the candlestick speak to her but it would not. Angrily she struck it and broke it in two, then ran from the room.

The next day the manikin asked to be put under the chair. The boy again tried to make the princess talk to him and again she refused, sitting stubbornly in stony silence.

"If you will not entertain me, then I'll talk to the chair," the boy exclaimed

and, after slipping the little box underneath it, he asked the chair to amuse him with a story.

The chair began: "A carpenter, a tailor and a holy man were once traveling together when they came to a dangerous place. They decided that two should sleep while the other kept guard. The carpenter watched first and he occupied himself by making a doll out of a piece of wood. Then the tailor took over and he dressed the doll to cover its nakedness. Then the holy man woke to keep guard and he took the doll, thinking, 'How beautiful she is! But she has no soul.' So he prayed to God to breathe a soul into the little girl. When all three were awake and saw that she was a human being, each one tried to claim her as his wife."

At this the chair paused and asked the boy, "Now, who do you think should marry her?" And the boy answered, "Why, the holy man of course." But before he could continue, the princess interrupted.

"What rubbish you speak! The carpenter must claim her, for if he hadn't made her in the beginning, she would not have existed at all." To the amazement of the judges, she went on chattering about the story. The judges quietly slipped out of the room and reported to the king that his daughter had spoken on the first two days.

After the boy had fallen asleep, the princess tried to hold a conversation with the chair but it remained silent as before. So she struck the chair and smashed it in pieces before dashing from the room.

On the third day the manikin said, "Tuck me inside your turban today. I will be safe there."

When the princess came into the room, she refused to speak despite the boy's entreaties. "Well, if you will not talk to me, I'll talk to my turban," he said. "Now, my turban, we don't want a story today; we want action – some dancing perhaps."

From underneath the turban there suddenly appeared a troupe of girls

dancing and playing castanets and drums. The boy started to enjoy the music, until the princess cried out to him to talk to her. "Why should I?" the boy replied. "I am being so well entertained by these lovely ladies."

The judges dashed off to tell the king and he came running in to see with his own eyes that his daughter was actually begging the boy to talk to her.

All were delighted with the turn of events. The boy and the princess were married and in time inherited the kingdom. The boy could now return to the merchant, having more than redeemed his father's gifts.

Believe me: I was there and saw it all happen!

THE FIRST CORN

CHIPPEWA (NORTH AMERICAN)

In far-off times a very poor man lived with his wife and children. His oldest son, Wunzh, was kind like his father and everyone loved him.

One day his father said to him, "My son, it is time for you to go on your spirit quest." Together they built his lonely lodge, and he cleansed himself and entered the lodge to begin his fast.

For two days Wunzh wandered through the forest, listening to the birds and observing the plants around him. He grew more and more curious about the plants, how they grew in the wilds and which ones were good to eat. But he soon became too weak with fasting to do anything but lie still and ponder these mysteries. "The Great Spirit made all things and we are grateful," he thought. "But life is still very hard, for we cannot always find fish in the waters, and our hunting sometimes fails."

Suddenly he saw a young man coming down from the sky, dressed brightly in green and yellow with feathers on his head that waved as he moved. He said to Wunzh, "I have been sent to guide you by the Great Spirit, who has seen your kindness. You can bring help to your people if you fight with me."

Though he was weak, Wunzh wrestled with the visitor, straining every muscle to match his strength. At last the young man said, "That is enough, my friend. You are weak, but you have done well." As he left the lodge he said with a smile, "I will return soon."

The next day they fought again, and this time the boy had even less strength. But his courage and his hope gave him a little energy and he struggled till he had no more breath. "That is sufficient for now," the stranger said, "but tomorrow I must challenge you again." With that he left the lodge and Wunzh collapsed on the ground, exhausted.

For the third time Wunzh wrestled. He was determined to win even if he should die in the struggle. He fought mightily until the stranger panted, "Wunzh, you have conquered me. Now let us rest and talk."

Wunzh listened intently to his visitor's words: "This is the sixth day of your fast and all is not over yet. Tomorrow your father will offer you food, but you must fast a little longer. I will come again if your strength prevails and wrestle for the last time. If you win our contest, you must take my clothes from me, sweep and soften the soil, and lay me down in it. After you have buried me in the earth, leave me in peace. From time to time you must come to check whether I have returned to life. Do not let other plants grow on my grave but put a little more fresh soil over me each month. In this way you will accomplish that which you desire." With these words he disappeared back into the sky.

Wunzh was able to refuse the food his father brought, even though the old man counseled him to take care of himself. Later that day, the sky stranger returned for the final contest. Wunzh was faint and starving but he fought with a mysterious new strength till his opponent lay dead. Then he took the young man's clothes and feathers and buried them, as instructed.

He went back to his family very weak. Slowly life returned to normal, but Wunzh often thought of his dead friend. Many a time he went to inspect the grave with hope in his heart. He weeded the ground and tended it lovingly till, one morning, he saw slender green shoots thrusting out of the soil. Each day he found them stronger and higher and he rejoiced silently.

By the end of the summer the plants had grown tall, with silken hair swaying from their tops like feathers. Wunzh decided to show his father, who was weary after an unsuccessful hunting trip. He was as excited and puzzled as his son when he saw the tall plants and heard Wunzh explain, "This is my friend, father, the friend of all our people. He is the spirit of the corn and he visited me during my fast. We may feed on this friend, as long as we cherish and take care of him, and we need not worry when we cannot find fish or meat." As he spoke, he pulled a stalk of corn from the plant and gave it to his father, whose tears fell down his wrinkled face.

"So this was the reward of your fast," he said to his son, "for the Great Spirit saw your kind heart and your courage."

Before they ate the corn, they thanked the Great Spirit for his gift and the father praised the son's courage and generosity.

So the Chippewa people were given food by the Great Spirit and sweetcorn came into their lives.

THE LITTLE FROG

CHILEAN

There was once a rather mean king who had three sons, Pedro, Diego and Juanito. The boys were kept hard at work since their father would not fork out money to pay laborers. But they grew weary of such treatment and, being curious about the world, they decided to set off to see how people lived beyond their father's lands.

The king was angry, insisting that they had not yet proved themselves, but he could not stop them from going. He only insisted that, in one year's time, they must all come back to him bringing a large measure of silver.

The eldest left first and before he had been on the road for long, he heard a voice singing most beautifully and he traced it to a poor cottage beside his path. He spoke roughly to the old man who sat outside the door. "Is that your daughter I can hear singing? For if it is, I must marry her if she is unmarried."

The old man replied sadly, "Yes, that is my daughter you can hear and she is yet single, but she cannot marry."

Pedro was annoyed with such a response, crying out, "Why not, you buffoon? I am a prince and I will marry her. Call her out to me at once."

The old man called to his daughter, then sighed as a little frog hopped out of the house and sat on the path in front of the prince. Pedro was so disgusted that he yelled, "So, you would waste my time, you wrinkled thing. Get out of my way!" And he kicked her aside.

Diego set out next and he, too, was arrested by the beautiful song that floated out from the cottage. He asked the same question of the old man and got the same response. "What do you mean, she cannot marry me? I am a prince and I will marry her if I want to. Command her to come out immediately."

Out hopped the wrinkled little frog and sat on the path in front of the prince. Diego roared with laughter when he saw the creature. "What! You mean I have been fooled by this ugly thing? Be off with you!" And he kicked her even more fiercely than his brother had done.

The youngest prince set out last and he too stopped to listen to the singing. He dismounted and asked the old man whether the voice he heard was that of his daughter. "Yes, she is my unmarried daughter but she cannot marry you."

Juanito cried out, "I will marry her for the beauty of her voice and the loveliness of her song. Nothing shall prevent me." As he spoke, out hopped the little frog. The prince gazed down at her and, though he was crestfallen to see her frog form, he could not forget her song. So he called for a priest and they were married at once. And whenever Juanito was sad because of his wife's shape, she would sing to him to cheer him up.

So the year passed and the princes knew they must return to prove
themselves to their father. The two older princes had each found beautiful
wives for themselves as well as bags of silver. As they rode home, they passed
by their brother's humble cottage and laughed scornfully.

Juanito did not know what to do. He had won no silver. "Don't worry
about that," his frog wife insisted. "Just take some of that coal in that dirty old
sack and throw in a wood chip from the hearth." Juanito did so and, with a
despairing farewell, he set off. "Do not open the sack on the way," his wife
called after him.

The king was delighted with the silver brought home by Pedro and Diego.
"But where is yours?" he asked his youngest son, who stood by with a long
face. The brothers mocked Juanito as the king opened his sack but were
silenced when pieces of silver streamed out of it. "So that you can see your own

reflection, I have also brought you a shining chip of gold," Juanito explained as he picked it out from among the silver.

The king was overjoyed and, turning to his older sons, said, "See what your little brother has found!" Pedro and Diego were very angry and determined to catch Juanito out.

That Sunday, the three brothers returned to the king's palace and feasted in their father's banqueting hall. The two older sons could not stop boasting about their new wives. "My wife can weave like a spider," said Pedro. "Mine can embroider even more cleverly," said Diego. Their mother, the queen, then set up a test for them, giving each a piece of cloth and saying, "Each of your wives must sew a tablecloth for me."

Juanito was desperate. "How can a frog sew such a cloth?" he worried as his brothers galloped off before him, hurling insults as they went.

When he told his wife of his problem, she snatched the cloth from him
and tore it to pieces. "What nonsense!" she said. "Don't worry about a thing.
Just lie down and I will sing to you."

When the time came, fearfully Juanito prepared to leave for the palace
with his fragments of cloth. But as he bade her goodbye, the frog said,
"Juanito, take this little box with you. But don't open it on the way."

So he returned to the palace and saw the marvelous things his brothers'
wives had made. He handed over the tiny box to his mother and was as

astonished as she was when she opened it and shook out a beautiful tablecloth. "This is quite miraculous handiwork!" the queen exclaimed. "Never have I seen anything like it. I will keep this for my own table and the other cloths I will give to my servants."

The brothers were in a foul temper at this and reviled their younger brother all the more. "You little wretch, you frog husband! Go back to the mud where you belong, you idiot!" They resolved to triumph over him at the next test.

The queen's bitch had produced three puppies. She gave one to each son, saying, "Take this to your wife and she can train it."

Confidently Pedro and Diego took the puppies home, while Juanito fretted, "What can a frog do with a puppy?"

When he explained the task to her, the frog took the puppy and threw it against the wall, saying, "Juanito, this is nonsense. Just lie down and sleep." Then she sang her beautiful song.

When the day came to take the trained puppy to the palace, he was full of gloom. "What shall I do? My brothers will taunt me mercilessly now." But as he departed, the frog said, "You'd better take something with you. Here, take this tiny box and this tiny key to your mother."

His brothers called out for him to hurry as they rode past and Juanito followed as usual, arriving just as the two well-trained puppies were being shown off to the queen. She asked Juanito, "And what can your puppy do, little one?"

The poor fellow could say nothing but gave his mother the little box, drawing back as she unlocked it. Imagine his surprise when a little puppy jumped out, dancing on its hind legs while a white dove hovered above it!

The queen was thrilled with the dog's tricks. The little animal jumped up to sit contentedly on her lap, while the two older sons looked on in fury.

At this point the king announced to his sons, "Now I command you to bring your wives to court, for we must meet them in the flesh now we have seen how talented they are. I will expect you here for a celebration next Sunday. Do not fail me."

Pedro and Diego rushed off with glee, knowing the beauty of their wives. They taunted Juanito and he trembled.

When he told his frog wife of the summons to the palace, she said, "Well, we'll just have to go then. Don't even think about it."

Sunday came, the oxen were yoked to the old cart and they set off. Juanito fell asleep as they lumbered along, and when he awoke, he was amazed to see that, instead of an old cart, he was riding in a splendid carriage that was being pulled not by oxen but gleaming white horses. Sitting beside him was no longer a frog but the most beautiful princess, singing softly all the while.

When they arrived at the palace, the brothers were angry to see the grand coach, for they were expecting an old farm cart to bring the slimy frog wife to court. There was such pleasure at the arrival of Juanito with his lovely bride that Pedro and Diego were soon swept aside.

The king felt bewitched by the most beautiful of his three daughters-in-law as she offered flowers to him and his wife. After they had feasted, the king and queen danced while Juanito's wife covered her husband's chest with the bones left on her plate. The other two wives imitated her, not knowing why.

Then the king ordered that the wives should play and sing and dance. "Pedro and Diego's wives will accompany Juanito and his bride as they dance together," he proclaimed. The frog princess danced gracefully, scattering pearls and flowers around her. The other princesses tried to do better, but as they danced they scattered horse manure instead.

Pedro and Diego were sulking. "Why on earth didn't I take the ugly frog?" Pedro cried out. His brother agreed, "Yes, what fools we were to miss such a chance."

At the end of the third day of feasting, the king announced, "Now I know all I need to know and I am going with Juanito and his wife to visit their home. I will ride with them." So off they all set for the frog wife's cottage.

However, the cottage was nowhere to be found and in its place stood the most magnificent palace, more opulent than the king's. Amazed, the king said to Juanito, "If this is your palace, then I have no desire to return to my own."

The princess, now free of her frog shape, could live happily with her husband till the end of her days, enthralling everyone with her beautiful songs.

MAUI-OF-A-THOUSAND-TRICKS

POLYNESIAN

When time began, Maui-muri lived on earth. Manu-ahi-whare was his father and Tongo-i-whare was his mother. The fire god, Great Tangaroa-of-the-tattooed-face, was their parent. Maui had two older brothers and a sister.

Each night Manu-ahi-whare slept beside his youngest son on his sleeping mat. Each day at dawn his father disappeared and Maui wanted to know where he went. He took one end of his father's maro* and lay on it so that his father would disturb him when he got up to dress. In this way he awoke and watched as his father chanted to the houseposts:

*maro: *sleeping mat.*

Open up to me, open up to me, you posts of the house,

For Manu-ahi-whare would pass through you,

To make his descent into the dark depths below.

In response, one of the posts lifted and Manu lowered himself down through the hole.

That morning Maui-muri told his brothers and sister to go outside while he hid inside. But instead of hiding, he also chanted to the houseposts:

Open up to me, open up to me, you posts of the house,

For Maui-muri would pass through you,

To make his descent into the dark depths below.

As he lowered himself through the hole, Maui took the form of a bird to fly to his father and then resumed his human shape. Manu was shocked to see his son there and they pressed noses in greeting.

Then Maui-muri went off to explore. He came across a blind old woman trying to pick up food. But she kept picking up burnt embers instead. He felt sorry for her as he stood beside four nono trees, watching her. Then he took a stick and struck three of the nono trees, the trees of his brothers and sister. When he struck the fourth tree, the old woman cried out, "Who strikes the sacred tree of Maui-muri in the underworld?"

"It is I, Maui-muri," he replied.

"Then you are my grandson," she said, "and I will make your barren tree bear fruit."

Maui-muri climbed his tree and bit a piece from an unripe fruit and threw it at the old woman, whose name was Hina-the-blind. It hit her in one eye and healed it. He threw another piece and gave back her sight in both eyes. With joy she sang:

All you find up above,
All you find down below
Will serve your sacred mana,*
Grandson of Hina-porari.

Then she gave Maui-muri sacred knowledge and answered his questions.

"Who is the god of fire," he asked, "and where can I find him?"

"He is your ancestor Tangaroa-tui-mata," she replied, "and he lives over there, my grandson. But he is an angry god, do not go near him or you will die."

But Maui-muri insisted on visiting the fire god, so Hina-the-old directed him. "There are but two paths to Tangaroa-of-the-tattooed-face. You must go by the common path, for the other is the path of dying."

Maui-muri took the second path and when Tangaroa saw him approach, he raised his right hand to kill him. But Maui-muri lifted his right hand also, and the god was surprised and raised his right foot to kick him to death. Then Maui-muri raised his right foot also, and the god knew that he was his grandson. They greeted each other and wept.

"Why have you come to find me in this dangerous place?" asked Tangaroa.

"I have come to find fire," the boy replied.

Tangaroa then gave Maui-muri a burning stick and he walked off with it. When he came to a river, the boy thrust the stick in the water and put out the

*mana: *supernatural or magical power.*

fire. Then he returned to his grandfather and complained that the water had
killed his fire. The fire god gave him another fire-stick and Maui-muri thrust
it in to the water again and killed the flame.

There were no more burning sticks left, so his ancestor had to get two
sticks to rub together to make more fire. "Hold the grooved wood for me, my
grandson," said the god, "so that I can twist the sticks in it." But when Maui-
muri held the wood, he blew and blew on the tinder and blew it all away.

Tangaroa was angry and asked his special bird, his white kakaia, to help
instead. The tinder smoked and then it was fanned to flame. The fire was
made. Maui was jealous of the fire god's kakaia and he took a charred stick

and marked the face of the lovely bird. Such was his mischief.

Maui-muri offered to show his grandfather Tangaroa the world of light. "I will lead the way," he said. Then he flew high up in the shape of a bird.

Maui-muri dressed his grandfather in the glorious girdle of the rainbow and by its mana he rose up into the world above, to the top of the highest coconut tree. Maui-muri flew below his grandfather, not beside him, and when they passed through the clouds into the open sky, he pulled the cord of the girdle of the rainbow and Tangaroa-of-the-tattooed-face fell to his death. Then Maui-muri was able to return to earth with his ancestor's fire.

He showed his people how to make fire with two sticks, so that they might cook food. They were all very happy with the gift of fire, but Maui-muri did not tell them he had killed the fire god.

His parents wanted to visit the old man too, but Maui-muri persuaded them to wait till the third day. Meanwhile he descended again to Tangaroa's world and found his body decaying. So he put it in a coconut shell and shook the shell, rattling the god's bones inside it. When he opened the shell, his grandfather was whole and alive again.

On the third day Manu and Tongo went to visit Tangaroa. They greeted him and wept, but his mana was lost. He complained, "Your son Maui-muri is the culprit! He scorched the white face of my bird. He made me fly and killed me. Then he put me in a shell and rattled my bones. And now I am alive again, but very feeble. Your son is full of mischief."

It was Maui-muri who first gave us fire so that we need no longer eat raw food. He also slowed the sun so that we have more daylight in which to work. But that is another story!

THE KING'S VINE

SERBIAN

Once upon a time there was a king who had a remarkable vine in his garden, where he loved to sit in thought with a glass in his hand. From time to time, he would pick a few grapes and press their juice into his glass, filling it with sparkling wine that gladdened his heart.

One day, when the king went into his garden, he was horrified to discover that his precious vine had disappeared. His heart ached for his plant. Immediately, one eye filled with tears, though the other continued to shine with joy. When he returned to his palace, his son was most concerned to see his father's state.

The king said sadly, "My son, my heart is sore, for my vine has been stolen. Though one eye will always remember the joyful hours I sat beside it and drank its juice, the other eye will forever weep for its loss."

The king's son loved his father dearly and knew how painful it would be for him to grow old without the comfort of his vine, so he decided to go at once in search of the lost plant.

"Dear father, I will find your vine and bring it back to comfort you in your old age," he vowed as he waved goodbye.

He traveled far till he came to a forest where he sat down to rest and satisfy his hunger. As he opened his pack, he heard a cry of pain from a fox caught in a trap. He set to work to release the poor animal and then offered him something to eat. The fox wanted to know where the young prince was going and was told the story of the vine.

"How lucky that we have met," said the fox, "for I know where the vine is. It will be dangerous to retrieve it, but we will travel together and I will help you."

They journeyed on for many days till they came to the gates of a garden. Then the fox stopped, saying, "This is where you will find your father's vine, but you must do exactly as I say. You will pass twelve guards before you reach the vine. If their eyes are open, you may proceed, but if they are closed, hide from them, quickly. You will find two spades beside the vine, one of gold and one of wood. Use the wooden one to dig up the plant and hurry back to me."

The prince did as the fox said and all went well until he grew tired of the wooden spade and took the golden one to dig the ground. But as it hit a rock, it rang out so loudly that the guards came rushing to the vine. They captured him and took him to their master.

The master mocked the youth, then said, "But don't worry. I will let you have the vine back if you will fetch for me a golden apple from which I can grow golden trees in my garden."

With this the prince left the garden and told the fox what had happened. "I can help you again," said the fox, "for I know where such golden fruit can be found. But you must obey me this time."

The youth was most grateful and they traveled on till they came to another garden, where the fox again stopped, saying, "Here you will find the golden apple. Once more you must deal with the twelve guards. By the tree you will find a club of gold and a club of wood. Use only the wooden one to shake the tree and come back to me with a golden apple."

The prince passed by the guards, hiding from those with closed eyes and ignoring those with their eyes open, so that he came safely to the tree. But when he saw the two clubs, the golden club seemed far more suitable to knock down a golden apple, so he took it up and struck the tree. Immediately the noise of gold on gold echoed through the garden and the guards came rushing up to take him captive again.

This master also mocked his efforts, but reassured him that he would allow the youth to keep a golden apple if he could find a golden maiden and bring her back to his garden. With these words, the young man was released.

"If only you will help me again," he begged the fox, "I will certainly obey you this time."

"Very well," said the kind animal, "but we must now go to the third garden. You must deal with the guards as before in order to reach the golden maiden, who is guarded by an ugly and dangerous old woman. She will offer the maid to you, but you must refuse. You will see a long crook on the ground. Quickly pick this up and use it to hook the maiden and run off with her, carrying the crook with you."

When they reached the garden, the prince did as he was told. He was able to refuse the old woman's offer, but he hooked the maiden round the waist with the crook and drew her to him. Away they ran.

The couple met the fox and as they traveled back to the master, the prince grew sad at the thought of parting from the golden maiden. The fox felt for the youth and said, "Perhaps I can change myself into a golden maiden and you can exchange me for the golden apple."

The prince was most happy to hear this and laid the crook down on the ground as the fox instructed. The animal then jumped over it three times and

turned himself into a golden maiden. Then they set off for the second garden. The true maiden hid and the prince and the fox-maid were taken to the master.

The master mocked the youth yet again and said laughingly, "Well, I'd better reward this fellow for his efforts! Let us go to find a really big golden apple for him."

With the apple in his pocket, the prince quickly left the garden and found the golden maiden. Before long, the fox caught up with them, having shocked the master and his guests by changing into a fox and racing out of the garden like the wind.

As they traveled back to the first garden, the prince realized that the golden maiden was becoming very attached to the golden apple, so that she did not want to part with it, in exchange for the king's precious vine.

The prince confided in the fox, saying, "Dear fox, you have done so much for me. Now I am again distressed, for I must disappoint either the golden maiden or my father."

The fox reassured him, "I am sure we can work something out. Perhaps I can change my form again and become a golden apple! Put the apple on the ground and let me see."

With that he jumped over the fruit and became a golden apple. So the prince was able to give the true apple to the golden maiden and he took the other to the master of the first garden.

When he saw the prince, the master exclaimed to the guests who surrounded him, "What a clever fellow to bring me this golden apple. I had better reward him, since I always keep my promises."

So the prince was allowed to dig up the vine and he set off with it as fast as he could. He called the maiden from her hiding place and they went on their way, being joined very quickly by the fox, who bounded up to them and described the amazement of the master when the golden apple suddenly turned into a fox!

"Now we can part," the fox said to the prince, "for your task is finished and I can go back to my lair among the green trees."

"Dear, dear fox, I am so grateful for your help and I am sorry to lose you," the prince wept. "If you need me, I will always help you."

With these words they parted and the prince took the golden maiden

back to his father's garden. There he planted the vine in exactly the same spot as before and left the golden maiden to tend it while he went to find the king.

The king was overjoyed when he saw the vine. He put his glass under the tree where it filled with wine as before. He drank with joy and embraced his son. The prince noticed that the eye that had wept since the theft of the vine suddenly dried and was laughing with the other eye, quite merrily.

Then he called his father to follow him to the golden tree which hung with golden apples, beside which sat the golden maiden.

With a glad heart the prince said, "My father, the tree is for you, to give you pleasure as you grow old. The maiden is to be my wife, to be my companion throughout my life."

The king was delighted and embraced them both. Then he went into the palace to arrange a great wedding feast for his son and his bride. After the festivities were over, the king again took refuge in his garden, sitting deep in thought beside his vine, while his son began to rule the kingdom with kindness and wisdom. Together they would wander in the garden and the golden bride would sit beside the old king. Then the king's son would fill her lap with golden apples and they rejoiced, along with all the people in the land.

THE SMITH
AND THE FAERIES

SCOTTISH

Long, long ago in Scotland, a strong-armed smith lived with his only, motherless, son. He was a slender, dreamy boy, but he worked hard with his father at the forge. All the neighbors feared for him, for the little folk loved such children, and they urged the smith to take very good care of him.

"Don't take your eyes off your boy," they said, "for the faeries will steal him and take him off to the Land of Light. Just be sure that you always hang a branch of the rowan tree over your door at night to keep them away!"

Each day at dusk the rowan was hung above the door and the boy remained safe, until one day the smith had to go on a journey.

"Don't forget to hang the branch before you go to bed," he warned his son before he set off. But of course the lad was too tired to remember, after his full day, doing the chores and roaming over the moors in the sunshine. When the smith returned, he found the door swinging on its hinges. He went into the cottage calling out to the boy and a thin voice replied.

"Father, I'm sick in bed. I must stay here until I am well again."

The smith was most distressed to hear this and to see the poor boy, so pale and feeble, aged by sickness, it seemed. He lay there helpless for days, only rousing himself to eat. The smith was puzzled that he ate so much, being so ill. He worried until one day he called in a wise old man to give him advice.

"This creature is not your son," the old man said, after he had seen the boy. "This is a changeling left by the little folk when they carried off your son."

The smith was in despair. The wise man comforted him and then said, "If you want to see your son again, you have a difficult task ahead of you. But first, go into the house and spread empty eggshells on the floor beside the fire. As the changeling watches you, pretend that these are heavy as lead, so that he becomes curious about what you are doing."

The smith did exactly as he was instructed, straining under the weight of eggshells until the changeling laughed out loud and screeched in his high voice, "In all my eight hundred years I've never seen anything so foolish!"

When he heard this, the wise man told the smith how he was to get rid of the changeling: first he was to light a fire near the bed and wait till the changeling asked what he was doing. At that moment, the smith was to grab him and toss him into the fire.

The smith did as he was told, throwing the creature into the fire just at the right moment. With a fearful wail, the creature was spirited out through the

smoke hole and disappeared suddenly into the cloudy sky.

When he heard this, the wise man said, "Now comes the difficult task, my friend. Now you must go right into the green hill to find the faerie lair. Only at full moon will you find the door into the earth. Take with you your Bible, your dirk and your cock that crows at morn. Do not fear the dancing and singing in the bright light under the hill, but enter boldly, sticking your sharp dirk into the doorframe so that the door cannot close behind you. Go right in to the faerie realm, protected by your Bible."

The smith waited patiently until the next full moon, growing more and more anxious about his boy. His heart ached to see him again and his courage grew along with his pain.

Once again the smith followed the wise man's advice and found himself on the hillside in the moonlight, listening to the sound of music coming from beneath his feet. Suddenly, a great light shone and the earth opened up before him. With the cock under his arm and Bible in hand, he stuck his dirk in the doorframe and went into the hole in the hill. He found himself in a huge room, at the end of which he saw his own son working at the faerie forge. To reach him he must walk through the dancing green folk. He must resist the dance, for if he were to get caught up in it as a mere mortal, he would be forced to dance forever. As he drew near to his son, he saw that his eyes were wild and his lips were pale, driven to work the forge by faerie magic.

The little folk were furious that a man should dare to trespass into their hiding place under the hill and they challenged him angrily. But he moved through their midst and answered their challenge as the wise man had instructed him. "I have come to find my son and I will not leave without him," he said.

The faerie folk looked menacing as they tried to get near to him, but the power of his Bible kept them at arm's length and the smith was able to reach his son. As he did so, he cried out in his booming voice, "Release my boy from your spells at once. Release him, I say, and let him come home to his own country."

When the boy heard his father's voice, he was overjoyed. His eyes grew calm and he stretched out his arms to his father. At once the faerie folk shrieked aloud and mocked the daring of the smith. At that moment, the first light of morning touched the hill and the sleeping cock woke and crowed mightily at the coming of the light.

In terror, the little folk responded, for they must not let the light into their dark hiding place. They rushed to close the door into the hillside. However, the dirk in the doorframe prevented them and the smith and his son were able to get by. As they escaped, the mortal man drew his knife from the doorway and they ran for the safety of morning.

An angry faerie creature cursed them as they fled, crying out, "You may get home but your son will never speak again until my spell is broken."

With that the door closed on the faerie hill and the sun shone over the moor. Great was the boy's joy to find himself in his familiar world once more. He roamed the moors again and helped his father at the forge. So they would have lived contentedly, except that the poor boy could not speak a word.

For a year the smith and his son lived in peace. Then, when a year and one day had passed since his rescue from the faerie people, they began to make a

rich sword for the chief of their clan. It was to be a particularly splendid sword and they were excited by their work. Wordlessly, son and father labored with the molten metal as the sun rose in the sky, and they worked as the sun fell down behind the western hills.

As the boy worked, a sudden image flashed into his mind. It was a strange memory of the fire of the faerie forge. Then he caught a glimpse of the little folk and heard the spells with which they tempered their metals and the passion with which they hammered their shining blades. The smith watched in amazement as his son's hands worked the metal, his eyes shining strangely and his lips beginning to move with the rhythm of his hammer. So he worked until the most magnificent sword was finished, a weapon like the faeries' own. The boy smiled as he saw his father's admiration.

Triumphantly, he said, "Father, here is a blade that will never fail. He who fights with it will never be defeated!"

He spoke. The spell was broken. Unknowingly, he had fashioned his own magic cure as he made the faerie weapon. The boy lost all memory of the little folk and their dancing under the hill. He grew and prospered, becoming the most famous smith in all Scotland. His faerie sword brought his chieftain great glory and for his clan it won honor and fame.

THE STOLEN CROWN

DALMATIAN

Once upon a time there lived a king who had three sons, each of whom he loved dearly. One day he went out hunting with his chief minister and when he became weary the king lay down in the shade of a huge tree with his crown on the ground beside him. He soon fell asleep. When he awoke, he reached for his crown but it was nowhere to be found. The king searched, his minister searched and all his huntsmen scoured the forest, but to no avail.

The king was so angry that he condemned his chief minister to death for not protecting his crown. He was of course quite innocent, for the thief was the Fairy Alcina, queen of fairies. Since he was ashamed to appear without his crown, the king hid in his chamber and refused to receive anyone. His sons were puzzled by his behavior and the eldest said, "I cannot understand why our father should conceal himself. He must be sick or upset, so I will go and comfort him." However, as soon as he entered the chamber, the king shouted and hurled one of his boots at him. The eldest son beat a hasty retreat.

The middle son heard his brother's tale and said, "It is my turn to go to our father, to see if I can help him." But he fared no better than his brother.

It was now the turn of the youngest and favorite son, Benjamin. "I will go to our father and see whether he will speak to me," he said.

When the king saw him, he relented, saying, "I cannot speak even to you! For what has happened makes me feel such shame and embarrassment."

Benjamin replied, "But, father, how can we help you if we do not know what troubles you? If you won't tell me, I'll kill myself, for I can't bear to watch you suffer so."

The king could not endure such talk, so he told his son all that had happened, making him promise that he would not tell his brothers. Immediately Benjamin recognized the work of the Fairy Alcina and cried out, "I will seek her out wherever she is and retrieve your crown, or die in the attempt."

Benjamin took his horse and set off at once. Soon he came to a place where the road branched in three directions. A signpost pointed down each path, the first saying, *"Whoever follows this path will return."* The second sign read, *"There is no way of knowing what will befall the one who goes this way."* The third sign said, *"Whoever follows this path will never return."* Benjamin set off a little way in each direction before choosing the third road.

The path quickly became rough and he was pestered by insects and snakes. Finally it was so bad that his horse would go no further, so he said goodbye to it and continued on foot. For many lonely miles he walked, till he came to a cottage. Feeling faint with hunger, he knocked on the door and asked for food.

An old woman appeared, asking, "Why are you here in this dangerous place?" Before he could reply, she went on, "I am the mother of Bora, the Northeast Wind, and if my daughter sees you, she will devour you. Nevertheless I will bring you something to eat."

While he ate he told her of his quest to find the Fairy Alcina and recover his father's crown. The old woman could not help him, but said that her daughter would know who and where the fairy was. So she hid the prince under the bed and urged him to be quiet while she fed her daughter. The Northeast Wind soon returned, ravenous and raging and demanding food. With each mouthful she grew quieter and by the time she had eaten her fill, her mother was able to tell her about the visitor and made her promise not to harm him.

Benjamin crept out from his hiding place and Bora was quite kind to him. She informed him that on her travels she had seen his father's precious crown, lying with a shawl of stars and a musical apple of gold on the bed of the Fairy

Alcina. "The apple and the shawl were stolen from two queens whom she has imprisoned down a well by means of a magic spell," Bora explained. "I will tell you where you can find these queens and the Fairy Alcina herself."

Benjamin was delighted with the news and the Northeast Wind promised to give him a potion to put the watchmen to sleep. "Then you must enter the grounds of the palace of the Fairy Alcina and find the gardener," she added.

"But how will I deal with the gardener?" Benjamin asked anxiously.

"Do not fear," the wind answered, "for he is my father. You may take an introduction from my mother."

The young prince set off and did all that he had been told to do. He drugged the guard and gave his introduction to the gardener, who then offered to help him. "You will have to dress as a gardener to get past the two Moors who watch over the Fairy Alcina. They are commanded to kill anyone who enters the palace, except me when I bring her flowers."

So Benjamin impersonated the gardener and entered the palace carrying a huge bunch of roses. He found the fairy sleeping, so he took the crown, the musical apple and the shawl while gazing down at her beauty in amazement. He felt compelled to kiss her, but the apple made a sound and he fled, fearing that she would wake. He left the palace with no idea that he had been close to destruction, for anyone who dared to kiss the Fairy Alcina was turned to stone!

Benjamin walked for many hours and eventually came to a deep but dry well. It was so deep that daylight could not reach even halfway down. As he was peering over the edge wondering how he could descend, a wild goose circled overhead. It offered to let Benjamin climb on to its back and then it flew gently to the bottom of the dark well.

There the prince found the two queens huddled in the darkness. "I have come to free you," Benjamin exclaimed, "and I have recovered your starry shawl and your musical golden apple. So climb upon the goose and we will return to the sunlight."

The goose soared up and up and out of the well, over the land and forests until it reached the place where Benjamin had left his horse. Gratefully he bade farewell to the goose, greeted his horse and mounted with the two queens behind him. The horse then galloped back to his father's palace.

When his father saw his crown safely in the hands of his youngest son, his joy was boundless. He made Benjamin kneel down in front of him. Then he lowered the golden crown onto his son's own head, saying, "You have won this crown. Now the crown and the kingdom are yours." Benjamin chose one of the queens as his bride, they were married in splendor and, as far as I know, they are reigning still.

THE PRODIGAL SON

BIBLICAL

There was once a man who had two fine sons, both of whom he loved dearly. The young men helped their father run his large estate, along with many servants who worked the land and took care of the animals. They lived together contentedly, until the younger son began to feel restless and impatient with his life.

One morning he confronted his father with the words: "Father, I am weary of my life here, doing the same work day in and day out. I want adventure and excitement! Please let me have that part of your fortune that you planned to give me one day, and let me spend it on those things I long for now while I am young."

The father was sad to think that his son wanted to leave home already and, although he felt it was perhaps too soon or unwise to part with the money, he did as the lad asked and divided their inheritance between the two sons.

The young man was soon ready to leave and set off in high spirits. He traveled at speed till he came to an exciting foreign city, where he began to enjoy himself, living in luxury and spending his money on every pleasure he could think of. He drank and partied all night and slept all day until he was quite exhausted and not at all certain that he was actually happy. After some time his money began to run out, but he took no heed until his last coin was spent. He was hungry but had no money to buy a meal and no one to turn to: all his party companions who had lived so riotously with him now deserted him in his hour of need.

There happened to be very poor harvests that year and everyone in the city also had to go hungry as there was too little food to go around. Before long the young man was starving and trudged wearily from farm to farm looking for any kind of work that would pay just enough to keep him alive. When he could scarcely stagger any further, a farmer offered him work looking after his pigs. The boy accepted the job, even though he had to sleep in the pigsty with the animals. As he poured their food into the trough, he was often so hungry that he even ate the pigs' bran.

One day, as he tended the animals, he suddenly realized how foolish he had been. "Here am I, dying of hunger in a strange country, when the very least of my father's servants has decent food and lodging. My father provides for them all." He grieved at the thought of his father and his brother at home. After his stupidity, how could he ever face them again? "I have scorned their love," he thought. "How could my father ever forgive me? I have lost everything he worked hard for. I have wasted my inheritance."

The more he pictured his father at home, the more he longed to see him again. "I will leave here at once and return home," he determined.

The young man could wait no longer. He set off immediately for his own country and his father's lands, aching to set eyes on his family again. He walked for many days, till his legs could scarcely carry him, remembering the excitement he had felt when he traveled this path many months ago.

During his absence the boy's father had missed his son dearly. Each day he longed to hear some word from his child, hoping that his adventures had brought success but wanting, above all, to know that he was well. As he was walking through the ripening corn in his fields one day, he saw a figure moving slowly along the horizon. Curious, he watched intently as it came nearer. No one but a father could have recognized his child from so great a distance! The old man threw up his arms in joy, exclaiming to all the workers, "It is my son! My son has returned home!" And he hurried as fast as he could across the fields in the lad's direction. As soon as they met, the boy fell on his knees, saying, "Father, I have been foolish and irresponsible. I have dishonored God as well as you. I am not worthy to be called your son any longer. Treat me as no more than a servant, but please receive me home." But his father picked him up and embraced him joyfully crying, "Welcome home, my son. Welcome home!"

By the time they drew near to the house, the father had already issued orders for the servants to kill a calf, so that they could celebrate the homecoming at once. He had also noticed his son's tattered clothes and bare, blistered feet and the famished look on his thin face. So he sent at once for clean and splendid clothing for his boy; sandals for his feet and rings for his fingers. So great was the father's delight and so forgiving was his heart.

Before long the music was playing, the tables were bending under their weight of food; everyone was singing joyfully, all ready for the feast.

The older son was returning home after his day's work when he heard the celebrations and wondered what could be happening. A servant ran out to him, urging him to hurry home for his brother had returned unharmed. As the older brother took in the situation, he grew bitter. When he reached the house, he drew his father aside and cried, "I have stayed here with you, my father, faithfully working hard on your estate. Yet never have you even offered me a party such as this. But my brother, who ran away with his part of the fortune and squandered it all shamefully, is being feasted like a king!"

The old man drew his dutiful son to his heart and embraced him "My son," he said. "I love you very specially and am truly grateful for your faithfulness. But I had thought that your brother was lost, perhaps even dead! Yet here he is, alive, come back to us safe and sound. How can I not rejoice? Come, rejoice with me! For my son, your brother, was dead, and is now alive. He was lost, but now he is found." Then, arm in arm, they went to the feast, to celebrate together the return of the prodigal son, the boy who had gone away rich and come home in poverty to his father's love.

NOTES

SONS AND FATHERS

In these tales the mother is absent or her presence minimized. The focus of attention is the father–son bond and the development of the individual masculine personality and collective masculine values. Such energy is necessarily initiating and dynamic, but it must not be lived one-sidedly.

SONS AND BROTHERS

Where the stories portray the common unit of three sons, it is always the youngest who achieves most, in accordance with the wisdom that development usually comes from the inferior and least expected place. Fairy tales do not enforce our educational philosophy that we should build on strengths, but rather advise that we should attend to weakness. The fact that the last-born thrives questions the priority given to the first-born in most societies. Fairy tales commonly champion the disempowered. Where two sons form the sibling unit, they are usually polarized. The prodigal son, for instance, contrasts with his brother who is more cautious and apparently loyal to his father. We might also consider him to be more compliant and dependent. In "Maui-of-a-Thousand-Tricks" and "The First Corn," there is a larger family unit from which the special son is singled out, for he has powers that must serve the larger community. This is often the situation of the culture hero, who is marked for special tasks.

THE SON AS THE ONLY CHILD

Four stories present the fates of only sons, who are particularly subject to the father's influence, which is both beneficial and dangerous. The only son is given much attention for which there is no competition. The most supportive father ("The First Corn") can facilitate great things, enabling his son to struggle with nature itself (in the form of the corn spirit) to wrestle food from the earth. In "The Royal Candlestick," the father would be endlessly supportive of his much-loved only child, but spoils the boy, preventing him from developing any sense of self-reliance. It is only when outside forces intervene, in the form of the little manikin, that disaster is averted and the boy is able to learn such self-reliance and achieve success.

In "Daedalus and Icarus," Daedalus' craft and ambition are destructive for his son who is pulled into his father's orbit before his own strength has been kindled; Icarus simply admires his father's handiwork and lives from his energy. When he does finally get into the air, he cannot cope with the freedom and power he discovers. His father's warning has no force; the risk is too tempting and another boy falls from the skies.

In "The Smith and the Faeries," the smith, whose exceptional son is stolen by the little folk, pursues the lost boy into the faeries' lair to rescue him. He is then able to feel delight when the son's own skill exceeds his own, perfected by his experience at the faerie forge. Here, the father loses the son through a moment of negligence, sometimes a necessary "window" through which new developments can come.

FATHERS AS KINGS

To rule one's kingdom is to take possession of one's own life fully, with wisdom and authority; it is to *govern* without needing to *control*. A son who inherits his father's kingdom is taking his place in the succession of life, bringing fresh vigor and a renewed purpose. At a collective level, he is taking over the received wisdom and culture of those who have come before him. His task is to supply what is lacking and preserve what has value. The son must do, act, perform, in order to balance the ageing father's task of reflection and preparation for the eventual ending of life. Each individual, be he peasant or lord, needs to feel crowned monarch in his own being. Such is the metaphor that sustains so many of the tales that survive throughout the world, down through the centuries.

The father-king who tests his three sons wisely, proves them ready or unready to take on the responsibilities of kingship. He seeks to disclose values and motivations that will serve the kingdom. The foolish king who loses his crown and then blames others for the loss ("The Stolen Crown") clearly needs to hand over power, and it is his youngest son, for whom he feels most affection, to whom he can confess his folly and from whom he can receive help. The sons of the dying king ("The Water of Life") demonstrate their personalities in their motivation for renewing his life. It is dangerous when ambitious sons need the father to die in order to feel their power. But it is the youngest son's love that motivates his search, not his desire to disinherit his older brothers. When an ageing king ("The King's Vine") suffers the loss of his precious vine, the son sets off to redeem it. Great treasure is brought back to this kingdom, all the gold gathered on the son's journey. The rich associations of wine suggest how much has been lost to this kingdom, which the son must revitalise for the next generation.

SYMBOLS OF THE MASCULINE

In these stories we encounter masculine energy that is searching and proving, laboring and fighting. Daedalus, for instance, is the great craftsman who invents a machine for flying, suggestive of spiritual and intellectual aspiration. (Masculine determination and ingenuity are represented in this flight to freedom, though flight can also suggest loss of connection to the earth.) As Icarus discovers, it can also be destructive as well as progressive.

Fire and the forge unite father and son in "The Smith and the Faeries;" fire, evoking energy and life, and the forge bringing us in contact with force and muscle in the creation of metal implements and arms. The use of metals marks a vital stage in the evolution of civilization and the smith has always had a powerful aura, often associated with the magical. However, such weapons must be in the service of justice and tempered by love. In "The Water of Life," the youngest son wins a sword and a loaf, both of which he gives to a king who is vulnerable, so that he can defend his kingdom and provide for his people.

Masculine vigor and strength are needed to cultivate the land in "The First Corn." The young boy wrestles with the forces of nature to produce a supply of food. So the corn becomes a rich symbol of masculine labour and survival, a secret brought to fruition by the son, supported by a wise father.

The background to "The Prodigal Son" is also agricultural; the sons work on their father's land for provisions. The boy is reduced to the status of a hungry pig, sleeping in the sty, perhaps representing neglect of the responsibility to cultivate and ensure that life is sustained.

The crown, symbolizing power and authority, must be guarded and protected. Failure to do so puts masculine virtue at risk. When it is devalued, it is stolen, to be retrieved by the son who values it appropriately and is able to redeem its power ("The Stolen Crown").

The gold that appears in these tales is to be understood symbolically rather than literally; it suggests those things that are of highest value in the kingdom of the mind, the heart and the soul. Gold must be honored not exploited and, when necessary (as in "The King's Vine"), wooden implements must be used and the gold refused. When the true bridegroom goes to claim his bride, however, he must declare love's value by riding boldly up the middle of the road of gold to the princess's castle ("The Water of Life").

THE TEST

The father's expectations about his son set up trials which the son must pass or fail. These sons do not win victory by mighty deeds, but by demonstrating the right attitude to the creatures and situations they meet. They must survive on the road and in unknown forests, hungry and alone, or accompanied by strange companions. Although the sons may not realize it at first, the quality they most need to develop is wisdom. This is associated with being able to improvise, to do/make what is required out of the basic things each day offers. Such wisdom often lies in the feminine part of the psyche. In these tales it appears as gift from fox and frog ("The King's Vine" and "The Little Frog"), overlooked by the young men who are less in touch with nature.

The sons must also value music and song; they must be compassionate and generous, releasing foxes from traps and sharing their food; they must give priority to dialogue, asking questions and seeking answers. It is crucial that young men learn how to feel, without sentimentality. They must honor promises and commitments and they must be willing to be ruthless at such times; for they may be required to fight and kill a spirit-friend when he requests that ultimate act. Such tales present conflicts of values and test the wisdom acquired in the struggle for maturity.

Some sons seek out their own tests. They may be challenged by their father's sickness to find a cure, or by his carelessness to find his crown. The son lays this task on himself, even if his father resists. The motivation for the quest is crucial, sometimes contaminated by sibling rivalry or greed. Such motives are then exposed and are not allowed victory. Treasure must be won, not gained by theft; the sons who stole the water of life from their brother are exiled, while other competitive brothers simply lose energy and fall into oblivion by the end of the tale. The test for the older "good" brother of the wastrel, who stays at home with his father, is to participate in the celebration for the safe return of his prodigal brother.

SONS AS HEROES AND TRICKSTERS

The path of fairytale heroes is very different from that of the traditional superman who rises above the ordinary. They have a tricksterish capacity that allows them to make the most of circumstance. Just as one needs to descend a deep well, a goose flies by and offers its back for a downward flight ("The Stolen Crown"); another is assisted by a wise fox just when help is needed.

Maui manages to acquire fire from the fire god by a consciously wrought trick, just as he had achieved the healing of his ancestor's blindness. There is a special kind of knowledge hidden in these incidents and a special kind of cunning. They are very conscious acts that suggest an uncanny knowing of the mysteries of life that must be put at the service of humanity. Yet these tricksters are often disarmingly complicated and mischievous, and we sense that they are potentially dangerous and need to be treated with caution.

Tricksterish young men solve the puzzles set them by means of a wit derived from parts of the personality that are as yet undeveloped. Such is the help of frog, fox, or a little manikin who can hide himself in candlesticks and turbans. The hero must be able to cooperate with these special powers if he is to arouse speech in silent princesses ("The Royal Candlestick").

Animals and Brides

The strong and healthy king must also have a queen; so the winning of the bride implies readiness to inherit the crown. This is particularly necessary when, at the outset of the tale, the incumbent king himself has no queen. Many of the tales end with the winning of a bride, which also indicates the rounding out of the personality and its bid for wholeness.

Princesses are sometimes imprisoned in darkness down wells or in their own silence in a castle hedged by the skulls of beheaded princes. The princess's energy and speech must be released or the kingdom will remain deficient. The capacity to integrate feeling and instinct is often associated with the initiation of the relationship of the prince to the bride, who is rarely won directly. She is usually discovered as the journey unfolds. When the feminine has been trapped in darkness, like the queens in "The Stolen Crown," they must be released by the questing son and brought back to bring the feminine quality of feeling to the kingdom.

The son who is motivated by the need for power most needs to relate to his healthy instinctual life. He needs humility before natural life – offered to him, for instance, by the frog in "The Little Frog." The frog also carries aesthetic value; her song calms and inspires with its beauty. Lust for power always ignores this source of richness, which civilization needs as much as masculine-inspired technology.

Independence

Folk wisdom requires that dependent boys become autonomous men. Leaving home is a prerequisite for such autonomy and this departure must be timed right. The son must refuse his father's provision, when it is offered to keep him at home, no matter how loving the father's generosity. And the journey must begin even if resisted or refused by the father, for help is only available once on the open road. Then it is essential to treat the road and its wayfarers with respect. Only when independence is won, can the inner kingdom be ruled wisely.

SOURCES

DAEDALUS AND ICARUS
Apollodorus, Homer, Ovid.

THE WATER OF LIFE
Grimm, J. and W., *Grimms' Fairy Tales*, 1812–15.

THE ROYAL CANDLESTICK
El-Shamy, H. M., *Folktales of Egypt*, Chicago University Press, Chicago and London, 1980.

THE FIRST CORN
Clark, E. E., *Indian Legends of Canada*, McClelland & Stewart, Toronto, 1960.
Schoolcraft, H. R., Algic Researches: *Indian Tales and Legends*, Clearfield Co., Baltimore, 1992
(reprint of 1839 edition).

THE LITTLE FROG
Pino-Saavedra, Y., *Folktales of Chile*, University of Chicago Press, Chicago, 1967.

MAUI-OF-A-THOUSAND-TRICKS
Alpers, A., *Legends of the South Seas*, Thos. Crowell Co., New York, 1970.

THE KING'S VINE
Curcija-Prodanovic, Nada *Yugoslav Folktales*, Henry Z. Walck, New York, 1957.

THE SMITH AND THE FAERIES
Wilson, B. K. *Scottish Folktales and Legends*, Oxford University Press, London 1954.

THE STOLEN CROWN
Calvino, I., *Italian Folktales*, Harcourt Brace, New York, 1980.

THE PRODIGAL SON
St Luke, 15: 11–32.